P9-ANY-212

To all those who bring justice and beauty to the world — D. C.

To Rivala Garcia, Gwendolyn Pieper and Asa Core-Benson,
my young art students with the vision of Isabella — A. C.

SteinerBooks
610 Main Street, Great Barrington, MA 01230
www.steinerbooks.org

Library of Congress Cataloging-in-Publication Data
Roses for Isabella / illustrated by Amy Córdova;
written by Diana Cohen.—1st ed.
p. cm.
ISBN 978-0-88010-731-0
1. Roses - Juvenile literature. I. Title.
BT660.G8C67 2010
232.91'7097253—dc22
2010032329

Printed in China

Roses for Isabella

Written by Diana Cohn

Illustrated by Amy Córdova

Afterword by Lynn Lohr for Fair Trade USA

SteinerBooks

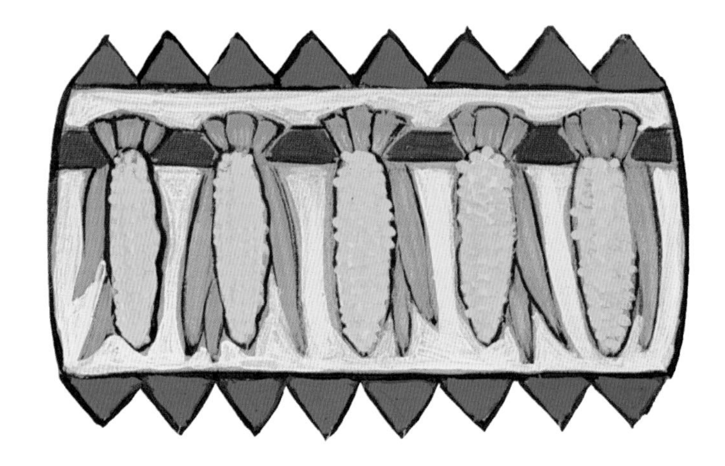

This morning, Cotacachi, the volcano that watches over my village is veiled in clouds of white, as soft as the wool my grandfather spins.

After breakfast, I get ready to walk to school. Mama weaves my hair into a long braid and ties it with a brightly colored ribbon.

Papa watches me put my writing book into my schoolbag. He says with a big smile, "Isabella, you are our family's first writer."

¡Vamos a Escribir!
¡Let's Write!

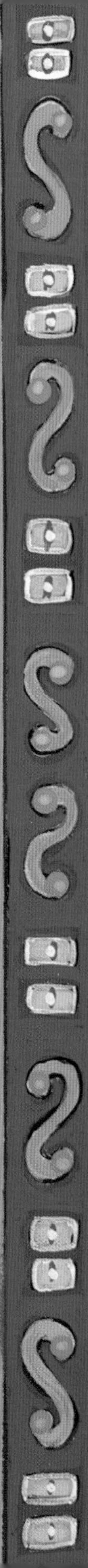

My teacher Miss Lopez has a surprise for us today.

"We will have a special assembly soon to honor Pachamama, our Mother Earth. You will all write stories, and one of you will be chosen to read your writing at the assembly," she says.

More than anything, I hope it will be me. What shall I write? I sharpen my pencil, lean over my desk, and begin.

Ecuador

In my country the sun shines almost every day, all year long. That is why flowers grow so well here. My mama and papa have always worked on farms that grow beautiful roses.

Miss Lopez reads my first lines out loud. "This is a good beginning, Isabella, what will you write next?"

I tell her I want to write about the new flower farm where Mama and Papa work. Miss Lopez tells me it is important for writers to visit the places they write about.

"Perhaps I can take you to the farm one day after school," she says.

I'm excited when my parents agree to show me and Miss Lopez the rose farm.

Each day I wait to hear if I can visit the farm. Finally, the day comes.

The New Rose Farm

Pink, red, yellow, and orange roses grow in rows that go on forever. My favorites are the roses with yellow petals with fine orange edges. I tell Mama they are the color of sunrise.

In the sticky hot greenhouse Mama picks off all the leaves that aren't perfect. She wears a bright yellow apron and blue rubber gloves.

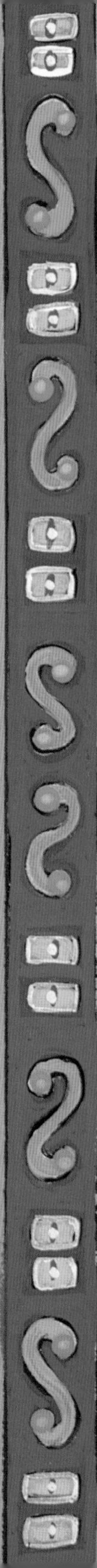

The Old Flower Farm

Mama got bad headaches and hot, red rashes at the farm where she used to work from the chemicals that were sprayed on the roses to keep the bugs away. Her headaches became so terrible, she had to stay home. When Papa asked the company to help Mama and the other workers who were sick, he was fired. I was sad because there was nothing I could do to help them. This was a hard time for my family.

The New Farm

One day, my Aunt Esperanza told Mama about a new rose farm that tried not to use bad sprays.

At first Mama didn't believe her, but she hasn't had one headache since she and Papa started working there.

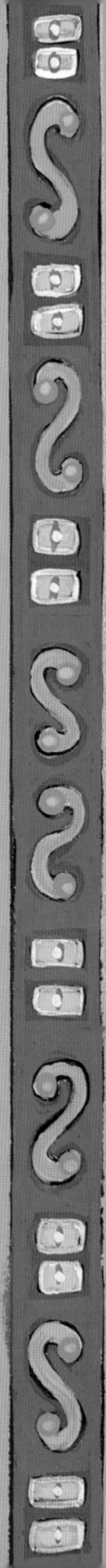

A Special Label

I visit Papa in the big cold room where he sorts the roses by their size and color. The rose stems are so long, they're almost as tall as I am! Papa packages the roses for their long airplane rides to stores all over the United States and around the world.

Papa puts a special "Fair Trade" label on each package. The label tells everyone that the roses are from farms that are cleaner and safer, and where the workers get paid better. The roses from the farm where Mama and Papa work cost a bit more, but that is why we could build our home.

Love and Roses

Mama and Papa work hard all year long, but they are busiest just before Valentine's Day and Mother's Day when everyone wants to buy roses for the ones they love.

Pachamama

At special times during the year we celebrate Mother Earth, Pachamama. We thank her for the rivers and the rich brown soil, and for all the food and life she gives us.

With all of our friends and neighbors, we give
Pachamama gifts of food and song and dance.
Mama tells me that Pachamama smiles when we
treat the earth and her people with care.
I think about the people thousands of miles away
who buy our special roses. I think they must
please Pachamama too.

The next day I write a poem. When I show Miss Lopez, she says, "This a beautiful poem, Isabella. Will you read it at our assembly?"

When I tell Mama and Papa my news, they give me a hug.

A few days later I read my poem. Everyone claps when I finish.

A better world is blooming!
When roses,
red and yellow
and other colors
of the rainbow,
are grown with care,
when those who grow them
are treated fair,
Pachamama smiles.
A better world is blooming!

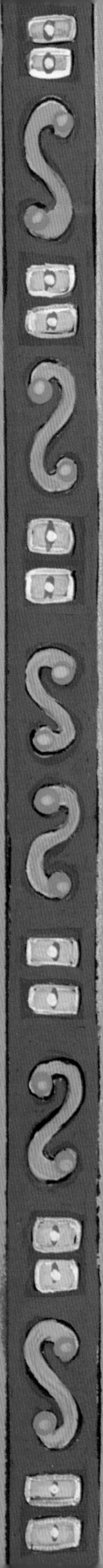

One day, Mama says, "Isabella, There is something special I want to show you."

We take the bus to the rose farm where I see a new sign that welcomes everyone who comes to work or visit. Painted in big, bold letters is my poem!

Papa has gathered together all the people who work at the rose farm.

"Isabella," Papa says, "We know these are your favorite."

Then Papa gives me a big bouquet of roses, the color of sunrise.

A BETTER WORLD IS BLOOMING!
When roses red and yellow and other colors of th
inbow are
grown with care, when those who grow them
fair,
PACHAMAMA SMILES!

Afterword

Happy stories such as *Roses for Isabella* are happening all over the world. Isabella's family is one of a million and a half families in Latin America, Africa, and Asia that are part of a sweeping global movement called Fair Trade.

Fair Trade was developed in Europe some years ago with the idea that farmers and workers in poor countries should be paid a fair price for the food they grow and the work they do, especially by those in wealthier countries like the USA, Canada, and Europe. In 1988 an organization in Holland decided to buy coffee raised by Mexican farmers who had only small plots of land. In the past, these farmers had been paid very little for their coffee — not a fair price at all! Together the buyers and the farmers worked out their own agreements and principles of Fair Trade. The farmers would be paid a fair price, based on how much it cost to raise their crops. In return, they would continue to take great care in how they farmed their land, so that the people, the birds and animals, and even the water would always be included in their care. They would support the shade trees that shelter their fields, and protect the rivers and streams that flow through their lands.

Soon other organizations and companies in Europe were buying from more and more small farmers, from Mexico to Malawi, and Chile to China. In 1998, people in the U.S. began to buy Fair Trade coffee as well. Today, farmers from more than 70 countries in the South sell to consumers in more than 20 countries in the North. And coffee was just the beginning! Now you can buy Fair Trade bananas, chocolate, rice, mangoes, and pineapples. You can also find Fair Trade sugar, honey, tea, herbs, spices, and more. Fair Trade ingredients are in everything from ice cream to hand cream. It's even possible to find Fair Trade sports balls and Fair Trade t-shirts. Soon, you might even be able to find a Fair Trade school uniform!

What is also so special about Fair Trade is that the companies, besides paying a fair price, put money into a community fund. Then, the groups of farmers and workers decide together how to spend the money. — "Should we build a school or a clinic ?" they might ask, or "Is it time to buy a new truck to get the sugarcane to the sugar mill more quickly?"

Sometimes, the funds are used to buy computers, or to take children on a special trip to a museum or to attend a soccer camp. Other times, everyone agrees to buy new little coffee trees for replanting, or to build a bridge across a river so no one has to go miles out of the way to get crops to market. Quite often, the money provides loans for workers to buy land or build a house. Once the loan is paid back, another family gets a turn.

How do you know if something is Fair Trade? You look for the Fair Trade labels. Below are the Fair Trade labels for the USA and Europe, Japan, and Australia. When you see them on a package you know that everyone is following the rules of Fair Trade. These labels mean that people are working together to protect the families of farmers and workers and the Earth. How can you be sure? Every year, a specially-trained person visits each Fair Trade farm or factory and goes through a long checklist as a test to make sure the system works.

How can you help? If you want to know more about Fair Trade and how you can get involved go to www.FairTradeUSA.org. The site belongs to an organization called Fair Trade USA that works to educate everyone about the whole idea of Fair Trade and to promote Fair Trade from one corner of the USA to the other. Purchases are choices. Your choices help to make things fair for families everywhere because every choice matters with Fair Trade.

Lynn Lohr, for Fair Trade USA

ACKNOWLEDGMENTS

A bouquet of Fair Trade roses for

Eduardo Letort, Rocio Giron, Vinicio Parra, Margarita Andrango, and Carlos Carrion, Lucia Carrion, Marcela Chorlango, Patricio Lechon, Angelica Jativa, and all the workers at the Hoja Verde and Joygardens flower farms who so generously gave us their time and feedback on this book.

A basket of Fair Trade chocolate for

Betty Sachs and Steve Juniper and everyone at Casa Mojanda in Otavalo, Ecuador; and Jaime Archino Arios Ayala, Ivan Suarez Procel, Miriam Ernst, Handel Guayasamin, Valentina Guayasamin, Eliza Chavez-Fraga and Janet Shenk; and Lynn Lohr, Laurie Lyser, Hannah Freeman, Kazuko Golden, Paul Alvarez, Stacy Geagan Wagner, Joan Catherine Braun, Paul Rice and Mike Conroy, and other staff and the board from Fair Trade USA for the work they do to promote Fair Trade and for all their logistical support and feedback on this book.

A package of Fair Trade coffee for

Craig Merrilees, Dan Enger, Oliver Kit McCreary, Lisa Schubert, Gene Gollogly, Mary Giddens, Amy Goodman, Jennifer Beckman, Ann Bastian, Nikos Valance, Edda Ehrke, Ali Ghiorse, Zoe Lane, Hans Schoepflin, and Molly Sims for all their support along the way.

ABOUT THE AUTHORS

Diana Cohn (l) and Amy Córdova (r) with Marcela Chorlango, President of the Workers Committee, the committee in charge of representing the rights of the workers on the farm.

Diana Cohn is an award-winning children's book author. For over two decades she has worked on environmental, economic, and global justice issues as a teacher, a media activist, and a program director for foundations with social change philanthropy missions. Her books include *Namaste!* and *Dream Carver* with Amy Córdova, as well as *Yes, We Can! Janitor Strike in LA*, *Mr. Goethe's Garden*, and *The Bee Tree*. She lives with her husband in northern California.

Amy Córdova is an artist and storyteller, whose art reflects soul and spirit. She has been recognized for her work as an illustrator of children's books, including the Wisconsin Library Award for *Namaste!* and honor winner of the American Library Association's Pura Belpré Award 2009 and 2010. Amy lives in Taos, New Mexico.

Lynn Lohr is a Fair Trade Certified activist and a former teacher and theater artist. She is Executive Director of the Consultative Group on Biological Diversity (CGBD), an international membership organization working to conserve and restore biological diversity. She worked for the Foundation for National Progress, the publisher of *Mother Jones* magazine, to develop support for investigative journalism and has produced professional theater doing all new work based on history, folklore, and social issues. She lives with her husband, Lance Belville, in Sausalito, California.